William Wallace Everts

Through the Narrows

William Wallace Everts

Through the Narrows

ISBN/EAN: 9783744758598

Printed in Europe, USA, Canada, Australia, Japan

Cover: Foto ©Andreas Hilbeck / pixelio.de

More available books at **www.hansebooks.com**

IN THE HARBOR.

Narrows.

Through the Narrows

BY

REV. W. W. EVERTS, D.D.

" Life is a bark borne by the gentle gale,
Freighted with hopes, to some far distant clime."

NEW YORK
ROBERT CARTER & BROTHERS
530 BROADWAY
1884

THIS PARABLE OF LIFE

IS DEDICATED

TO PARENTS, TEACHERS, AND GUARDIANS;

AND TO

THE THOUGHTFUL CHILDREN

THEY ARE SO ANXIOUSLY AND HOPEFULLY

SEEKING TO GUIDE ON

THE VOYAGE OF LIFE,

BY

THE AUTHOR.

PROEM.

---◦◆◦---

FORTY years ago, on a Sunday School picnic to Fort Hamilton, New York Bay, where the channel formed by the confluence of the East and North Rivers finds its outlet to the ocean, as the steamer bearing the excursion was rounding into the stream to return to the city, the pastor was called upon for a speech. As he stepped upon the bench encircled by the guard of the boat and looked upon the children crowding the deck before him, the channel filled with vessels around him, the spires of the city dimly seen in one direction and the expanding ocean in another, and the setting sun gilding land and sea, the scene was picturesque and inspiring. This parable of life then flashed upon his mind, and "Through

(5)

the Narrows" is now offered to the public.
To blend the instruction of biography with
the pictorial interest of parable, we have
cited examples of eminent men in illustrating and enforcing the principles and promise of early training.

W. W. EVERTS.

January, 1884

CONTENTS.

PROVISIONS OF VOYAGE.

Through the Narrows.

"Train up a child in the way he should go, and when he is old he will not depart from it."

The waters washing either shore of Manhattan unite at its southern extremity, and sweep away in a broad and majestic stream, to the ocean. Grouping the most picturesque scenery with the most resplendent monuments of civilization; furnishing an outlet to the noblest bay; and opening a highway for the world's commerce,—this is one of the most interesting channels of the sea. Compared with the breadth of the ocean, stretching away so many thousand miles from its expanding outlet, it has been called the Narrows. In its relation to the harbor and the sea it suggests our parable—the Voyage of Life.

I.

" Swiftly thus our fleeting days
Bear us down Life's rapid stream."

A VESSEL freighted for a foreign port passing down this channel does not re-pass it next day. It seeks remote seas and has begun a long voyage. So child-hood furnished with ancestral traditions and hopes glides down the Narrows bound on the Voyage of Immortality. Early years are not taken up in repe-titions of experience, but stretch on to new experiments, measure succes-sive stages of progress, and connect themselves with the remote destinies of unending being. Childhood is a fresh morning flower sultry Noon has

(11)

not withered, evening frosts have not nipped, and violence has not crushed. It is a rivulet rising amid picturesque mountains, meandering through the valleys and staying not in its course till swelled by tributaries, it disappears in the ocean! It is a traveler, not tarrying at inns: but holding on his way, till leagues, the breadth of a continent, or the diameter of the globe, separates him from the point of his departure! It is a bark of faultless model, anchor weighed, helm set, and white sails inviting breezes to waft it across the seas. It is gliding down the "Narrows," seeking a remote and uncertain haven! This ceaseless progression is less observed because a generation move together, like drops blended in a mighty river. But the elastic step of childhood once lost is never regained. The col-

or faded from the cheek of youth is never restored. The hopefulness of manhood long repressed is never re-kindled. The eye dimmed by shadows of age is never reillumined. The inscription of years on the wrinkled brow is never effaced. Yesterday we gazed on the sunny countenance of a child, dandled him on our knee, and placed our hand on his head with benedictions. To-day he is a schoolboy seeking rewards of merit or contending in athletic games. To-morrow he will be a stalwart man pursuing agriculture, manufactures, commerce, a profession, or politics. Next day with bent form, dull eye, and piping voice, he is pitied as a relic of the past, or borne silently and tearfully to his burial.

II.

THE COMMON LOT OF CHILDHOOD.

" Survey the globe, each ruder realm explore;
From Reason's faintest ray to Newton soar—

. . . .

What slow gradations in the scale of mind !
Yet mark in each these mystic wonders wrought,
Oh, mark the sleepless energies of thought !"

ALL vessels going to sea from this
harbor pass the Narrows. The fishing smack, small coaster, pleasure yacht,
merchant ship, and the line or war
steamer move in endless series,—side
by side,—keep the same channel, glide
on the same tide, catch the same breeze.
Voyagers can see sailors pulling ropes,
or going aloft, on a neighboring ship,
and interchange salutations: so all em-
barking on the voyage of life pass the
Narrows of Childhood, restricted by its

(14)

ignorance, dependence, and helplessness. Newton's mind once inhabited an infant's frame. Shakespeare once looked out with the vacant stare of Infancy. Milton was once hushed to sleep by a mother's lullaby.

Prospective strength and weakness, wealth and poverty, learning and ignorance, virtue and vice, religion and impiety appear together undistinguished in the nursery, playground or school. The child who will be president of this Republic in 1900 is unrevealed to the most inquisitive prophets of destiny. Future Governors, Senators, Scientists, Philosophers, Poets, Philanthropists, Millionaires, are distinguished by no mystic aureole surrounding their brow. The future Arnolds, Burrs, Guiteaus, exhibit the same smiling countenance, buoyant spirits, and playful energy that charac-

terize other children. This common capacity and condition of childhood are
the hope of philanthropy and Christi-
anity. If the gnarled tree cannot be
reshaped by bending its trunk or in-
clining its branches and twigs,

> "A dewdrop on the baby plant
>   Has warped the Giant Oak forever."

If the majestic stream cannot be
turned from its course and made to
seek an outlet in another sea,

> "A pebble in a streamlet cast
>   Has turned the course of many a river."

Let parents praying for the welfare
of their children; Statesmen seeking
the glory of the Republic; and Philanthropists striving for the amelioration
of Society be cheered by the common
susceptibility and promise of Childhood!

Point out to the traveler his way in the morning, ere weariness come over his limbs, and discouragement over his heart, lest the day be lost in circuitous wandering. Go to the voyager before he has lost his bearings on the high seas: while he is weighing anchor, setting sail, present him compass and chart, and teach him how to hold the tiller.

III.

DIVERGING COURSES.

" Even a child is known by his doings,
Whether his work be pure and whether it be right."

VESSELS passing the " Narrows " traverse different seas, and reach widely separated ports. Some double Cape Horn, others Good Hope. Some cast anchor in Arctic, and others in Antarctic seas. Some make port on the shores of the Atlantic or Indian Ocean, others on the coasts of the Pacific. Passing down the *same narrow* channel abreast, exchanging signals, they separated at its outlet, and find Ports divided by the diameter of the globe. Such is the divergence of the destinies of Childhood born and reared in the same community. Those

(18)

who have played, attended school and church, together, remove to different parts of the country or seek their fortunes in remote lands. From the same youthful circle one rises to the pinnacle of Fame, another plunges into infamy; one boasts the distinction of learning, another is content with the obscurity of ignorance; one grasps power, another prefers the privacy of a citizen; one revels in wealth, another is straitened in poverty; one looks down from a Tower, another looks up through a Grate; one adorns society by his virtues, another blackens it by his vices. While Washington, Jefferson, Franklin, Adams, Webster and Clay rose to fame, their juvenile peers sank in obscurity. Those now holding positions of trust and honor have seen their early companions sink in discouragement.

At the commencement of this century
in one of the middle counties of the Empire State were two lads. One wasted
his superior advantages in idleness, and
dissipation. A few years ago he might
have been seen almost any day issuing
from the saloon of his native town, his
tattered garments and animalized features
disclosing his vices and his miseries. The
other acquired education, a learned profession, offices of trust, entered the legislative Halls of the State and of the
Union, and at length added the name
of Millard Fillmore to the roll of chief
magistrates of the Republic.

Thirty years ago an Attorney was
just rising into lucrative practice and
great popularity in one of the older
States. He was made governor of one
of the Territories, elected to congress,
and his victorious party seemed ready

to offer him any promotion. But the cup enthralled him. He drank under the table his political *confreres* in their revels. In a fit of delirium he leaped from a railroad train in his night dress. His junior of the same State, through the discipline of culture and piety, rose to various distinction in the public service and to the presidency of the United States immortalized by the Assassin's Pistol. In a Western State there appeared forty years ago two generous rivals at the Bar. Though natives of the same southern state, both espoused the cause of the Union in the Civil War. One became known as the War Governor and through superior talents and address might have attained any honor in the gift of the nation. But the cup degraded him and prematurely ended his popularity and his days together.

The other, with less culture, wealth, and social position through sobriety, industry, instincts of patriotism, and native force rose to be a peer of Washington. What possible destinies are opened to the millions of children now playing in our nurseries, or taught in our schools! An artist has represented the progress of life in two series of portraits. In one we see the child develop into the boy, ruddy and beautiful; the youth noble and aspiring, the man resolved and dignified; and old age serene and venerable. In the other series, the child is followed by the obstinate boy, the profligate youth; manhood irresolute and groveling; and old age, abject and despairing. The Missouri and Columbia rivers are traced almost to a common source. A traveler could drink from each the same hour. But flowing in opposite directions, they empty themselves into different oceans many thousand miles apart. So the little rills of humanity rising in common endowments and conditions of childhood, varied, widened, and deepend in their channels may issue in widely separated destinies of life and Immortality!

IV.

> " *As the sun,*
> *Ere it is risen sometimes paints its image*
> *In the atmosphere; so often do the spirits of*
> *Great events stride on before the events,*
> *And into day already walks to-morrow.*"

CARELESS observers see in the vessels passing down the " Narrows " in endless series, no signs of different destinations. But those noting the model of ships, their flags, their crews, and observing their course from the Hook, discover signs of differing destinations! So amid common aspects of nursery, school or play-ground, one may discern auguries of various manly character or destiny. We need not study palms, use charms, or incantations to foretell the probable destiny of children.

(24)

In the young forest the naturalist traces the future oak, pine, beech, maple, and among the scions of the Nursery he can tell the plumb, peach, apricot, or cherry. So vices and virtues of children may be anticipated; and their character and destiny shaped.

V.

THE idle are drones in a hive, depleting treasures they did not hoard: partners in a firm, whose capital they exhaust, but never replenish. They waste inherited fortune, and put forth no exertion to earn another. Neglecting work, they lose both tact and capacity for it, and gradually sink into hopeless poverty. Want of trade oftener than want of education betrays men into vagrant and criminal life. Of seven hundred and eighty convicts, under twenty-one years, in the Philadelphia Penitentiary, seven hundred and fifty-five had no trade:

while only one hundred and ninty-three had been denied the advantages of the Common School. A Jewish proverb says, " When a man teaches his son no trade; it is as if he brought him up to high-way robbery." But while idleness is losing, industry is winning all the prizes of life. Three fourths of those rising in professions or commerce were so distinguished by industrious habits, that their school vacations were devoted to some remunerative industry. "When a boy among my native hills of New Hampshire," says Webster, "no cock crowed in the morning so early that I did not hear him, and no boy ran with more avidity to do errands at the bidding of the workmen than I did." A family driven from England on account of their participation in the reform movements at the close of the last century, lost their fortune by bad investment in Baltimore. The oldest son, of only sixteen, with robust health and industrious habits, lessened the sufferings and helped to restore the fortunes of a large family. Seeking in New York as the commercial center of the New World employment as a manufacturer, he refused the more honorable and remunerative service of book-keeper that he might learn the trade. "Any one," he said, "might keep books: but he wished to learn a business." From the lowest service he soon rose to be foreman of a large establishment; then a partner; and in a few years the manufacturing house of William Colgate & Co. was known throughout the country. He commenced his independent business, without book-keeper, or porter, and closed his store an hour before the proper time that he might personally deliver the first goods he had sold, a mile up town. He said, every one needed daily the fatigue of physical toil. His industry supplemented by other virtues, gave him ample fortune, and made him the most distinguished benefactor of a large denomination. Trained in the same industrial virtues and enlightened views of the uses of wealth, his sons have attained foremost rank in business and philanthropy. Industry of the toiling brain or the sinewy hand is Carlyle's "escape from evil." Ruskin calls it the "door of good." Says Franklin, "if we are industrious, we shall never starve, for at the working man's house hunger looks in but dares not enter, for industry pays debts, while despair increaseth them." In our country there is no condition so low but that with associated virtues industry can not achieve wealth or competence. An Atalanta Journal tells of four lads in that city who sold newspapers for a living. To save a certain percent of their earnings, they went their morning rounds through snow and sleet of winter barefooted. While supporting invalid parents, when the oldest was eighteen and the youngest twelve, they owned a good home, several houses and considerable bank stock. Estates rising over the country from the smallest beginnings are the measure of the national earnings and multiplied memorials of the national industry.

VI.

THE prodigal child keeps nothing. He does not preserve the nuts or berries he gathers, or books given him. In youth his wardrobe, however frequently or generously furnished, always appears scanty and in shabby condition. From the earnings of later years he lays by nothing. If he inherit property it is soon covered with mortgages and he suffers in want As a clerk receiving scarcely enough wages for food and clothing, he spends a large portion of his small pittance in confections, cigarettes, and drinks. A manufacturer paid

seven hundred dollars of marked bills to
his employées Saturday night, and on
the following Monday morning found
four hundred and fifty of these iden-
tical bills deposited in the bank by
liquor sellers. A clerk was inveigh-
ing against employers for the scanty
salaries paid their clerks while he was
spending sixty cents at a bar treating
friends. It is improvidence that keeps
many poor among us though they are
clever, industrious and painstaking. Un-
less the poor husband their earnings they
can never gain wealth or even competence. Discontents, frauds, forgeries,
and wreck of character and domestic
happiness may be traced to the growing extravagance in personal and family
expenses. It has been said Germans can
live on what Americans waste; Jews on
what Germans waste; and Chinese on

what Jews waste. The superfluous expenditures of young men would suffice to support families with respectability. A child taught to husband his little earnings, in later years may lay by a portion of his annual income, and through life continue to add to his estates or his charities. A German youth came to New York at the close of the last century with the thrifty instincts of his native land. He availed himself of the extraordinary advantages opening in the Metropolis of the New World. He earned and husbanded his earnings. He rose above the technical merchant to be a trader in the products of industry and commerce. He established a Northwestern fur-trade and gathered larger properties from its continued enlargement. He invested his increasing wealth in real estate, chiefly in New

York. Endowed with all the industrial virtues, grasping the commercial
promise of the capital of the New
World, and living to a great age,
John Jacob Astor owned the largest
amount of Real Estate ever acquired by
one man in this country. His heirs,
honoring their traditional virtues, are
still the largest real-estate owners in
New York, if not in the New World.
Without industry and frugality none
can accumulate: with them all may
attain competence if not wealth. Fru
gality has acquired, and given per-
manence to, large estates; warded
poverty from barren lands; and filled
myriad homes of all ages with bread.

VII.

ECONOMY.

It is not enough to earn and husband
to prosper. One must also know how
to use. As well waste with the prodigal as hoard with the miser. It is the
skillful use of means that assures the
highest success. The bad player loses
the game to one with inferior hand;
the unskillful general the battle to one
not having half his battalions. Wealth
enough passes through the hands of
unwary speculators in Wall Street every
day to make thousands rich, but not
one in a hundred has the economy to
save a competence from that Waterloo

of Capital. A wealthy banker says any fool can make ten dollars, but only a wise man can make good use of five of them. Economy arises from a trained sagacity. A child taught to play, study and work with proportion and system may grow in skilled capacities, strength of purpose, and character, and become able to manage trusts of corporations, or of Civil Government, and project speculative enterprises to develop the resources of the country. One born in New York at the close of the last century, remarkably endowed with a genius for speculation which was fostered by the enterprise of a growing city and country, and operating in railroad and other stocks till an advanced age accumulated larger wealth than any other citizen; and bequeathed to the Vanderbilt name perhaps the largest

estate ever acquired in a single generation by a single family. Trained
economy, industry, and frugality divide
among themselves the wealth of every
land and age. A wary use of resources
has elevated the race from barbarism,
amassed the fortunes of the rich, furnished with elegance homes endowed
with limited wealth and adorned with
beauty the cottages of the poor.

VIII.

HONESTY.

THE dishonest boy cheats playmates in games or trades; takes things from home without permission; appropriates whatever he finds without seeking an owner; and robs gardens, orchards, and fruit stands. Following this penchant he will cheat in business, defraud an employer, or partner, or become a defaulter in public trusts. Temptations to dishonesty are more various, subtle, and persuasive through commerce, than through agriculture, manufactures, or professions. Through frauds

of commerce the community is educated
in every form of dishonesty.

The unscrupulous boy is sure to be a
dishonest man; and a thoroughly dishonest man is the contempt of the
world. Honesty nurtured in childhood
is the only sure support of upright character. The boy that returns the play-
thing he has borrowed or found to the
owner, when grown up will not embezzle
funds, take advantage of the widow and
orphan, or defraud an employer, or rob
a public treasury. Faithful in little, he
will also be in much, and will gain
promotion. A chimney sweep strug-
gling with tears against the temptation to take a watch exposed where
he was employed, won the favor of
his patron and gained a place above
his calling. Honesty in commerce is the
first condition of confidence, and suc-

cess; and honesty in commerce promotes it in every department of life.
The merchant that has scrupulously
maintained it through a long period
and a vast extent of business deserves
the distinction and praise of a public
benefactor. A north of Ireland boy,
with great sagacity and force of will,
began business in New York at the
beginning of the century as a pedler.
He soon became a merchant; and by
keeping familiar with the wants of his
customers, and the markets of the
World, the most assiduous devotion
to business, and scrupulous honesty,
A. T. Stewart became the greatest
and richest merchant in America, if
not in the World. He never lost
credit at the Banks; was never sued
for failure in a contract; never marked
his goods with two prices. A clerk

detected in misrepresenting the quality or price of goods was dismissed. A merchant going into bankruptcy without paying his creditors in full was refused credit in any new organization of business. All true and permanent commercial prosperity must be based on honesty. Dishonest gains neither impart credit nor happiness to their possessor, nor do they abide with him. Without the confidence based on honesty, accumulation is uncertain, or if casually acquired is soon lost, and entails greater poverty and misery. The dishonest speculator is always despised. But the declaration of the poet, " An honest man is the noblest work of God," is received with the currency and prestige of a proverb throughout the world. Giving credit to individuals, stability to

trade, security to investments and nobility to character, commercial integrity
is shown to be a universal duty, as
well as the highest expediency—" the
best policy."

.

IX.

GAMING.

It imparts an unhealthy stimulus to commerce, disaffects towards normal industries, and trades, and precipitates the rash speculations which wreck fortunes and families. More grain is sold annually in Chicago than is raised in all the world. Provisions and stocks are sold for future delivery and at speculative prices. A New York correspondent of a San Francisco Journal says that of the fourteen thousand brokers in New York not more than three hundred and forty really sell any stocks. William H.

Vanderbilt said before a Legislative Committee, " Not one man in ten entering Wall Street, is not a loser in the long run." This passion for gambling must be corrected in youth if at all. A leading merchant in Chicago determined to discharge all clerks who gamble in pools. Children should be taught to avoid all games of hazard. The smallness of the wager does not hinder the inoculation of the poison. The fraud essential in all gaming fosters trickiness, insincerity, hypocrisy, heartlessness, hatred. Making issue with the law of God and the conditions of all human welfare: it fascinates, enslaves, and makes men satanic. The gambler is a professional cheat and robber. He refuses to contribute to the great partnership of life. The gambler is not honest or just with God or men ! He would turn soci-

ety into a den of thieves! Why encourage by doubtful games or trifling
wagers, a vice so insidious, selfish and
destructive!

X.

TOBACCO.

This Narcotic, by vitiating the blood, and impairing the nervous tissues reduces the vigor of physical manhood; by encouraging improvident habits, lessens the promise of wealth; by stimulating disordered appetites, increases the power of temptation. A recent number of the Dublin University Magazine, voicing the scientific opinion of the world, gives this warning to parents: "The mental power of many a boy is certainly weakened by smoking tobacco. The brain under its influence can do less work and the dreary feeling which is pro-

duced tends to idleness." But perhaps
the moral peril is greater than the physical, or mental. Whatever economical
or social considerations may favor the
use of tobacco by adults, there is no
plausible reason for its toleration in
childhood or youth. Many parents in-
dulge while condemning the use in themselves; much more should they resist it
in their children. "No cigarettes for
boys!" is a warning now appearing over
some drug-stores. Let it be enforced
in every store, family, and school in the
country. It is already proposed for the
Statute books of some States; let it be
the law of every commonwealth! Through
early education the race may be weaned
from this expensive and dangerous luxu-
ry and aspire to purer and more elevating diversions.

XI.

THE cup develops an artificial taste into a tyrannizing habit, enfeebling the body; obscuring the intellect; mortgaging estates; entailing poverty; debasing character; and destroying the individual and the family. It fill**s** the ranks of inebriates, paupers, and criminals; ravaging society as the locusts did Egypt! It is a miserable fallacy that men must use alcohol in beverages moderately to become temperate! As well pretend they should use arsenic, prussic acid, or Paris green moderately in their food to show their wary self-control. Poison like sin should not be tampered with, but universally eschewed. Gen. K——, of a Western State, was a man of culture, elegant manners, and high social position. When he fell by the cup, friends expostulated with him for his own reputation, and the honor of his family. He confessed his imperious appetite. To their importunity he replied "It is vain! One of the most affectionate and noble wives in the world often pleads with me in tears. Sons and daughters of whom any one might be proud, joining their entreaties in vain! Why should you hope to be successful where such pleaders fail! No, I am helpless—lost!" In early life the bondage of vicious habits may be escaped. Admiral Farragut describes his triumph: "I accompanied my father as a cabin boy. I had qualities I thought made a man of me. I could swear like an old Salt; could drink a stiff glass of grog as if I had doubled Cape Horn; and could smoke like a locomotive. I was great at cards, and fond of gaming in every shape. At the close of dinner one day my father turned everybody out of cabin, locked the door, and said to me, 'David, what do you intend to be?' 'I mean to follow the sea.' 'Follow the sea! Be a poor miserable, drunken sailor before the mast, kicked and cuffed about the world and die in some fever hospital, in a foreign clime!' 'No!' I said, 'I'll tread the quarter-deck and command as you do!' 'No, David; no boy ever trod the quarter-deck, with such principles as you have and such habits as you exhibit. You'll have to change your whole course of life, if you become a man!' My father left me on deck. I was stung by

SHIPWRECKED.

Narrows.

the rebuke and overwhelmed with mortification. '"A poor, miserable, drunken sailor before the mast, kicked and cuffed about the world and to die in some fever hospital?" That's my fate is it? I will change my life, and change it now. I will never drink another glass of intoxicating liquors. I will never gamble!' And as God is my witness, I have kept those vows to this hour!"*

Let thousands on the verge of poverty, disgrace and hopeless misery through enslaving appetites rise to the heroic purpose and honorable life of the great . Commodore.

Bad habits are a satanic police marching generation after generation of the thoughtless and wicked to destruction.

* This and some other personal narratives we have quoted from Dr. Craft's "Successful Men," published by Funk & Wagnalls.

Good habits are an escort of angels guiding the wise and prudent in safe paths of life and convoying them to the better land.

XII.

SCIENCE, Philosophy, and Art do not arise from animalized childhood. Barbarism is the creature of instinct and passion, and flourishes in the eclipse of reason. Ignorance creates herded populations, not civilized States. Superior reason is the day-star of progress. When Alfred the Great was twelve years old, the queen mother offered a manuscript of poetry, she chanced to be holding, to the prince who should first learn to read it. The older princes had no ambition for the task or reward; but Alfred soon gained the prize. While he became the

(53)

most illustrious ruler and benefactor of the age, the names of his brothers faded out in the annals of undistinguished royalty.

John Stuart Mill at three years of age began Greek; at eight, having read Xenophon, Herodotus, Plato, he began Latin. In morning walks he told his father what he had read the day before in Robertson, Gibbon, Hume, Rollin, Plutarch, or Mosheim. The father would give forth ideas on civilization, government, morals, which the son had to ponder and restate in his own language. The boy had few if any playmates, and sought recreation by reading the " Arabian Nights " and similar works. By the time he was twelve he had read the Latin classics, gone through higher mathematics and begun logic. At eleven he wrote a history of the Roman Government, which showed democratic tendencies in the child's brain. At fourteen his father sent him to the schools and he became the most cultured and learned man of his time.

When a lad amid the hills of his native granite State, and his schoolmates were playing around him, Webster might have been seen under the shade of a tree near the school-house poring over the "Constitution" printed on a cotton handkerchief. Elihu Burritt, through greed for books and the public welfare, arose from the anvil to the highest rank of scholarship and philanthropy. Thurlow Weed's love of books was not repressed by poverty. When a lad he went several miles in winter with clouted feet to borrow a history of the Reformation. He became one of the most influential political writers of his time. Horace Greeley with similar tastes, and against similar disadvantages founded the New York Tribune, and became the greatest Tribune of the press. A few years ago a newsboy in Chicago through quick intelligence, industry and fidelity became a journalist. He became such an expert in railroad interests, he was employed as private secretary in one of the great railroad offices. No man in the country is now more conversant with the origin, history, principles and policy of the administration of these great corporations than J. M——. Though still young, he receives a salary rarely awarded to older men, in great corporations. He ranks as the second railroad expert in the country. He is summoned to railroad conventions; and his intelligence, testimony and judgment are sought in settling difficulties, fixing tariffs, policies, or terms of pooling the earnings of roads.

XIII.

THE average mind is constituted to follow, not to lead; to use discoveries, not to make them. If more prophets were needed more would be inspired. Prophetic gifts often appear in childhood. A lad delineating geometrical figures on the floor with chalk at six years of age: at twelve repairing toys for his playmates: at sixteen constructing electrical machines, and making experiments with the steam of a tea kettle: ultimately invented the steam engine and gave immortality to the name of Watt. At the age of six, before he could write the notes

(57)

on paper, Mozart composed pieces for the harpsichord, playing thus early to discriminating ears, preludes to the incomparable harmonies of his later years. West when a mere child, drew the likeness of a babe in the cradle so strikingly that the mother clasped him in her arms in ecstasy of delight. He used to make paint brushes from the coarse hair of a house cat: and when at length a friend presented him a set of brushes with paints he was so delighted that he kept them by his bed at night, and waking often put out his little hand to feel that they were there. Leadership in scientific art was forecasted in the tastes and habits of early years. Archetypes of the steam-engine, steam-boat, and spinning-jenny existed in the inventive brain of Watt, Fulton, and Ark-

right long before they were con-
structed for the world's use. The
history of electrical science gives us
three marked examples of the boy's
genius presaging the man's brilliant
future. Morse, the son of a clergyman, from childish studies and experiments worked up to the invention of
telegraphy. Edison while the train boy
was devising some new method of
signals, and publishing a little sheet,
afterward the terror of his fellow
workmen for his daring experiments,
but lastly a light bearer for the world.
Gray a poor boy was always planning
curious tests of power with open eyes
and ears for Nature's phenomena. In
maturity the vibrations along the metal
pipes of his bath room fell upon a
trained sense and the ready brain
worked out the wonderful telephone.

XIV.

THE coward has been despised in all ages, in all grades of civilization. Timidity in the presence of danger is tolerated only in an invalid or a woman Courage transfigures life with glory and gives a kind of sovereignty over human affairs.

The regal bearing of Cyrus in childhood gave him mastery over playmates, made him ·King of the shepherd boys, and pointed him out as a future ruler of men. The ·most illustrious of military heroes, when a

(60)

lad, had little fellowship with his companions: sought the seclusion of a solitary summer-house on the sea, listening to the breakers roar, and watching the sea bird's flight. A small brass cannon was his favorite toy, and mock military displays his greatest diversion. Daring traits exhibited in Nelson's youth in attacking a bear with the breech of his gun, in the Polar seas, and in volunteering to board a prize in a gale, gave promise of his renown as the first naval captain of his time. Lord Clive, the founder of the British Empire in India, when a lad climbed the church steeple of the parish; organized his schoolmates into companies, and proposed to the shop-keepers, for a small allowance, to protect their property. Resolution, pluck, daring, exalt one to leadership, and arm him for and emergency. A brave man is a host in any quarrel: a brave people invincible by any foe!

XV.

WITHOUT it individual man is reduced
to a Micawber, ever waiting for something to turn up; society to a railroad train made up, but without mo-
tive power. Our age is full of energy
dominated by evil or good purpose!
If instinct with selfishness, it is a
Jehu in destruction! Stirred by its
irresistible impulse, a New England
lad rose, through trading in knives
and the pedler's craft, to an interest
in stage coaches; steamboats; and rail-
roads; and at length became a stock
operator in Wall Street. He con-

(63)

tributed largely to the Black Friday
Panic, which seriously disturbed the
finances of the country. But while
rapidly accumulating wealth, he used it
only for personal indulgence, and am-
bitious display. He enlisted and splen-
didly equipped a regiment. He owned
an opera house and shamelessly associated with actresses and other women
of doubtful reputation. Brought into
conflict with those as base in character as himself, but cooler and more
calculating in their aims, he was at
length shot down, like a mad dog, in
a hotel in New York. The public
felt relieved of the most shameless
example of profligacy which has appeared in the social annals of the country. His energy was prostituted to the
demoralization of the country. He was
more dangerous to the morals of the

Republic than Catiline to the liberties of Rome. Another lad of New England ancestry, but born in a rough county of northern New York, exhibited the same indomitable energy with higher intelligence, a strong sense of duty. He taught a district school to obtain means for a fuller education, and assist in the support and education of his father's family. But the fall of Sumter interrupted his noble ambition, and called him at eighteen to defend the integrity and the honor of the Republic. He helped to raise one of the first and most distinguished cavalry regiments, and distinguished himself in all its battles. He rose from the ranks through several promotions for valor and discretion to captaincy. His further promotion was stopped by capture and fourteen months spent

in Southern prisons. After several
escapes, he was arrested, and confined
with more rigor, till he finally eluded
his guard and reached the Union lines
in Georgia. In his active mind all experiences, observations and studies of
the war were coined into literature.
He became the most popular historian
of the Rebellion. Hundreds of thousands
of his books were read in this country
and in Europe. In the national Cen-
tennial he crossed the continent on
horseback, stirring the nation's patriotism by lectures on "Echoes of the
Revolution." Subsequently he traced
the Mississippi to its source, which
his comrades named Glazier Lake.
These two exemplifications of American energy illustrate the glory and
shame of our country.

XVI.

THE irritable boy is fretted by every childish defeat, and disaster. In later life this unhappy temper clouds the sunshine of home, taxes the patience of family and friends, and repels strangers. Wealth cannot purchase for the ill-tempered man peace of mind, fellowship of friends, or sympathy of mankind. Byron's gloomy genius, soured it is true by deformity, was bred from childhood in moroseness. He scowled on the world with cynical prejudice; and disturbed its harmony with the loud notes of his hatred and

scorn. The boy of sunny temper,
though outrun in a race, beaten in a
game, or excelled in rank at school,
is still blithe as a lark, enlivening
every circle with his gayety, and awak-
ening complaisant regards in all by
his joyous spirit. In a juvenile band,
a lad of seven placed upon a bench
lustily beat the large drum, uncon-
scious of the music in his soul. But
the other boys, on small drum, fife
and tambourine, responded vigorously
to his time and created stirring strains
of martial music. So any true and
genial-hearted boy, expressing in the
freest manner his vigorous and joyous
life, awakens response in every circle
of childhood and contributes to the
glorious and prolonged harmony of
life! Sir Philip Sydney, whose dying
act of sympathy to a wounded soldier

on the battlefield alone would immortalize his memory, was distinguished by the cheerfulness and complaisancy of his manners, alike with the nobility to which he belonged, the circle of culture of which he was a distinguished ornament, and with the army whose courage and chivalry in foreign wars he illustrated. A sweet temper cheers as the sunlight or the songs of birds. A hopeful man is a universal benefactor. One never discouraged is the mightiest achiever!

XVII.

THE vulgar boy shows no deference to parents, or other superiors; no tokens of respect to equals; and looks with ill-bred contempt on supposed inferiors. His rudeness grows with his years into boorishness. He is at home in no re-fined circle; and suffers mortification for his ill-breeding all his life! The boy animated with the instinct of true po-liteness is deferential, respectful, or gra-ciously subservient to all about him. He does not omit morning and even-ing salutations to parents, brothers, and sisters; nor the greetings of neighbors

(70)

or strangers on the public streets; nor the respect due to the aged everywhere. He retains the manners of a gentleman through life. The mother of an American statesman learning that her young son had treated rudely the family grocer, led him back to the store and exacted an humble apology. It was a lesson of politeness for his lifetime. A business man gave three rules as essential to success in life. The first was civility; the second was civility; and the third was civility. Consideration for the claims of others should be enforced as one of the first and most important lessons of childhood. Rudeness, lacking the excuse of temptation, is the obtrusion of selfishness and the bluster of conceit!

XVIII.

WITHOUT it there can be no strong man or state; but one loses consistence of character and sinks into the tremulous instability of the jelly fish. He yields to the slightest pressure of companionship, circumstances, or casual temptations, as the weather cock to changing breeze. He is swept away by rising passion as leaves by a gust of wind; or borne along by force of prejudice to uncertain destiny, as driftwood on a swollen current. Having no fixed principle or purpose in life, one may take on from distorting influ-

ences a hideous expression of humanity;
as a clever artist shapes caricatures in
clay or on canvas. In feebleness of
conviction communities are swayed by
appeal of political or social leaders
as fields and forests bend before the
wind. They are "double-minded men
unstable in all their ways." But with
firmness one may breast any storm of
opposition; move against any current of
difficulties; and stand like a beetling
rock over the sea, calmly defying
dashing wave and wrecking tempest.
He follows without vacillation some
business, some party, and some faith!
His record is not a sandy shore sur-
rendering its identity to every recur-
ring tide! but a rock-bound coast lifting
the same immutable aspect to sunlight
and storm. No modern race has shown
greater tenacity of purpose, and force

of will, and heroic courage than the Netherlanders. Holding their besieged cities against Philip, without food, they were taunted with being " cat eaters and dog eaters." They replied with calm defiance, " Then know as long as ye hear a cat mew or a dog bark we shall hold out." They have defied the sea, and rescued their country from its waves. They were pioneers in the commerce with India. They established a navy at one time master of the seas. They withstood the diplomacy and armies of Philip, and the anathemas of the Pope, and laid foundations for the American Republic and the liberties of Europe. Error is better than lack of conviction; bigotry than persistent scepticism; fanaticism than hypocritical conformity; obstinacy than flabby obsequiousness. Firmness is essential to success alike in business, politics, and religion. As the Hebrew worthies were steadfast before fiery furnace and at the lion's den, so the Apostolic Church continued her testimony in the face of exile, the prison, or the fagot. And only as he is "steadfast and immovable" can any believer honor his profession by "abounding in the work of the Lord."

XIX.

WITHOUT a sense of it one neglects duties, glides into vices, and sinks into the instinctive life of the lower animals. He waits only temptation and opportunity to enter any career of brutality or crime! But with feeling of obligation unimpaired, a child holds a clue to guide it safely out of any labyrinth of ignorance or sin. If driven before a gale he has a compass to steer by, and a port to enter. He has principles which may restore lost fortune, credit or hope. Character is perfected by the trials of all honored trusts. Impatient of the stew-

(76)

ardship of Christ one falls into debasing
selfishness if not into a career of crime.
Loyalty to it exalts to rewards of virtue and eternal life. The discipline of
the Church is seeking to make all men
feel amenable to society and to God
for the use of their talents, culture,
and wealth. Conspicuous examples of
Christian philanthropy have appeared
in our country. Amos Lawrence some
years ago in Boston, and recently Peter
Cooper in New York, have pointed out
the safe and beneficent use of the growing wealth of our country. But two
business men of New York, members
of the largest religious denominations,
are so conspicuously honoring the stewardship of wealth that their names should
be repeated as an inspiring example!
G. I. S., the son of a Methodist clergyman,
and honoring his traditional faith, rose

through remarkable business capacity
to the management of one of the leading banks of New York. With increasing wealth his benefactions increased,
helping churches, private and public
charities, and educational institutions.
Though not reported rich he has become
the most conspicuous benefactor in a
large denomination. Within the last
eight or ten years his contributions are
reported at more than a million and a
half of dollars. J. D., a member of another denomination, attained a collegiate
education through extraordinary sacri-
fices, and entered the law. After the
fall of Sumter he hastened to the front
with the brave men of the Empire State.
Retaining his intellectual and professional tastes and Christian principles
unsullied through the war, he resumed
the practice of law in New York. He

sought a church home, as promptly as boarding place and professional office. He rose rapidly both in business and Christian reputation. Not satisfied with the Mosaic requirement of beneficence, he is reported to have pledged a fifth of his earnings, and to have greatly exceeded that proportion in his manifold charities. In personal contributions and influence he has been the greatest benefactor of one of the strongest churches in New York, the largest contributor to the endowment of a University founded by his denomination, and a generous giver to other institutions and charities. No Christian layman in this country, beginning without means, spurning stock speculations, and accumulating only by normal appreciation of real estate, is believed to have given so much, in so short a time, and from such moderate wealth.

The example of such men will help to solve the problem of capital and labor. It is exorbitant gains without commensurate charitable distribution that excites the envy of the rich and the hatred of the poor and precipitates the discontents, conspiracies, and reckless violence of Nihilism. Great accumulations would be tolerated with less impatience if they were in due proportion dispensed in private and public charities: instead of being all hoarded as personal and family wealth. The Christian stewardship of wealth observed would relieve every suffering class, endow every needed charity, hasten the spread of the Gospel, and conciliate human brotherhood in every land!

XX.

THE vindictive boy resents imaginary insults, quarrels with brothers and sisters, and schoolmates; growing up, he promotes altercations among companions, and murderous feuds in society. Professor Webster of Harvard years ago became angry with his creditor Dr. Parkman and murdered him. Before his execution his confession gave the key to his crime and his doom. "I was an only child, much indulged, and I have never acquired the control of my passions that I ought to have acquired early; and the consequence is this. A

(81)

quick-handed and brief violence of
temper has been the ruling sin of my '
life." The magnanimous boy does not
retaliate an injury or insult, return
blows, or bandy reproachful epithets.
By mild though firm protest he represses
anger in himself and appeases it in another. He becomes a peacemaker in
family, school, and playground. In later
life, always governing his temper, he
develops a more heroic character than
captors of cities, or conquerors of king-
doms. Peacemakers are exalted as "the
children of God."

"Great minds erect their never-fail-
ing trophies on the firm base of mercy."
Revenge is Satanic; forgiveness Divine.
Only by forgiving temper can the peace
of society be conciliated, or conserved.
"Hath any wronged thee? be bravely
revenged: slight it and the work is

begun, forgive it and the work is finished." In the daily prayer never omit the conditional petition—"Forgive us our trespasses as we forgive those who trespass against us"!

XXI.

UNTRUTHFULNESS embraces all inappreci-
ation of the truth as well as studied
hypocrisy and willful falsehood. It is a
mark of general depravity, and is con-
summated in diabolical treachery and
malignity. It impairs the confidence of
social intercourse, and political compacts,
and arms nation against nation. A
romancing child may become a prevari-
icating youth, a malicious slanderer, and
a perjured witness. Truth is the basis
of virtue, the cement of friendship, the
bond of society, the guaranty of con-
tracts and treaties. A boy scrupulous of

his word, and exact in his statements,
when grown up will not require wit-
nesses to his word, or bonds for his
promises. He may become arbiter in
individual disputes, and mediator in settling difficulties of corporations—or parties. "He that sweareth to his own hurt
and changeth not" in his incorruptible
truthfulness is assured of honor among
men, and of precedence and glory in the
everlasting Kingdom of God.

XXII.

THE disobedient child evades every commandment, slights every service, and ignores amenability to parents. In boastful independence he says of those to whom he owes his being and support in helpless infancy, "It is a gift by whatsoever thou mightest be profited by me." He naturally grows up impatient of authority, without respect for superiors, or old age. "The child is father to the man." Insubordination of parents forecasts a rebellious life and an evil doom. A brilliant woman ending a profligate career inadvertently disclosed the secret of its origin and consummation. " I never would ask forgiveness as a child; my father often tried and could not make me." Having refused obedience to parents one naturally refuses it to magistrates. Lawlessness in the home is followed by anarchy in the state. The foundations of civil law and order must be laid in domestic subjection. The obedient child may become the model citizen. " I should rather obey than work miracles," says Luther. " Honor thy father and thy mother" is the first commandment with promise. Filial obedience is specially honored by men and God. It presages the distinctions of personal virtue, the stability of the state, and the peace and happiness of heaven!

XXIII.

PRAYER.

PRAYER is conscious ignorance appealing to infinite wisdom for guidance; exposed weakness crying to listening Omnipotence for defense; imperfection deploring deficiencies, and seeking of the All-perfect One restored character and destiny; bowed sorrow looking up with tearful eyes to Him who has said—"Blessed are they that mourn, for they shall be comforted"; guilt, chastened by distressing apprehensions, pleading for mediation of infinite mercy; mortality, while stooping downward to the grave, lifting up its eyes to Heaven in vocal longing for immortality of being and blessing.

> " Prayer is the soul's sincere desire
> Utter'd or unexpress'd,
> The motion of a hidden fire
> That trembles in the breast !

> " Prayer is the simplest form of speech
> That infant lips can try;
> Prayer the sublimest strains that reach
> The Majesty on high."

Quarles says: " Heaven is never deaf but when man's heart is dumb." He that hears the ravens when they cry does not turn away from imploring helplessness, want, or woe. Though father and mother should forsake their offspring, God will never overlook the wants or be deaf to the prayers of His children. He who adorns the lilies of the valley, gives food to the birds of the air, and shelters and feeds the animal races in their various habitats, will hear the desire of the most humble, relieve their sorrow, sanctify to them their trials, and fulfill their hopes! An artist illustrates the guidance of prayer. A child following natural propensities is falling into the power of Satan, with malicious leer and weapon waiting to destroy it. An angelic messenger has descended, and with folded wing stands beside it, interposing a shield to turn its unsuspecting step away from danger, and direct its eye above. Yielding to a gentle touch, changing its course, and with clasped hands looking up to Heaven, the child is safe. No habit more effectually shields the young from temptations of passion, evil companionship, or proselyting error, than prayer. John Randolph said, "I am a French politician and I should have been a French infidel if my mother had not taught me at her knee to say, 'Our Father, who art in Heaven.'" Prayerlessness is an open door to irreligion and crime. The person or people, daily and devoutly repeating the Lord's Prayer, gain shelter from temptation, helps to virtuous dispositions and noble aims, and cherish promise of saving faith, and everlasting life. Over every condition of sin, sorrow, and despair is drawn by a Divine hand that bow of heavenly promise—"Whosoever calleth on the name of the Lord shall be saved." Then

> " Never, my child, forget to pray,
>   Whate'er the business of the day.
> If happy dreams have blessed thy sleep !
>   If startling fears have made thee weep !
> With holy thoughts begin the day !
>   And ne'er, my child, forget to pray."

XXIV.

FAITH.

Want of it leaves man maimed as loss of limb, or other bodily or mental or moral faculty. The loss of intuitive convictions of truth should be dreaded as distortion of mind or body. Rationalists assume that one of defined convictions is always narrow; one without fixed beliefs is the only broad man; and only one without any faith the truly rational man. But such pretentious sceptics are quacks in philosophy as well as iconoclasts in morals and religion. As no philosophy is more certain than the intuitive truths on which it is based, they would subvert the foun-

(92)

dations of all science as well as all religion. Agnosticism, without God and
without hope, is the harvest from the
seeding of boastful rationalism! Intuitive truth is like the sun. Without
that luminary our eyes would be of no
use. But if we gaze at that glorious orb
we are dazzled, neither seeing it nor
anything else. But as the race are
cheered and guided in their homes, and
in their daily pursuits, without compre-
hending the distance, magnitude, or com-
position of the sun; so intuitive revelation of God, the soul, moral law, and
heavenly promise, summed up in the
Christian annals, shine upon the minds
and hearts of men, vivifying moral sense,
illustrating and applying moral law,
and guiding them to perfected character
and happy destiny. Without religious
convictions and aspirations humanity is

left to fade with the flowers and perish with the birds. But, with superior sense of God, moral truth, and beauty, one is exalted to prophetic office, Christian pastorate and leadership. Samuel lay awake at night in the temple to hear the voice of God. He became the most incorruptible judge and one of the most renowned prophets of Israel. When a little boy, Robert Hall was seen listening as if hearing sounds in the air. Asked what he was listening for, he said, " I was trying if I could hear God in the sky." During the prevalence of a revival, a Green Mountain boy was observed sitting with his head against the wall and his eyes full of tears. His mother asked him why he was weeping. He said— " I was thinking I ought to go to —— (a noted infidel neighbor), and tell him the Bible is true." Nathan Brown we believe

wrote the missionary hymn, " My soul
is not at rest," and is filling out one of
the most brilliant chapters in the history
of modern missions.   All Christian ministry and missions arise from strength
of Christian convictions and eminency
of Christian love.   Undisturbed faith
in the Heavenly Father, and Divine
Saviour, will direct humanity to perfected character and happy destiny, as
infallibly as instinct guides the countless
myriads of beings in earth, air, and sea,
to food, shelter, safety and normal close
of their humble career.   The one who
does not encourage his child to trust in
God and repeat the Lord's Prayer is an
unnatural parent, unfit to be the mentor
of any human soul!   " 'Tis religion
that makes vows kept, transfigures life
with beauty and arches the future with
immortal hope!   Forty years ago I re-

ceived an apprenticed mechanic into the
fellowship of a Church in New York,
Christian experience and profession gave
a new impulse and direction to his life.
He rose from the skillful manipulations
of the humble artisan to the higher tastes
and pursuits of an artist. He went to
the front and attained military rank in
the Rebellion. After the War, along
with renewed devotion to art studies, he
took interest in politics, gained honorable public trusts, and received from one
of the great national parties a nomination
to Congress; subsequently he spent seven
years abroad perfecting himself in Art in
the galleries of Dusselldorf, Paris, and
London. F—— is now one of the most
accomplished Artists, orators, and lay-
preachers in this country, and his mature
years are crowned with usefulness, honor
and the hope of a blessed immortality.

Provisions of Voyage.

RESCUED.

Narrows.

XXV.

VESSEL.

A CALLING is chosen for a child as a vessel for a voyager. Abandoning a pursuit for which one has been trained should be as rare as leaving one ship for another in mid ocean. Great exigencies sometimes transfer a ship's crew or passengers from an imperiled to a safer craft. So doubtless, in the fluctuations of industries in a free and progressive age, change of calling may sometimes be safe and wise. But a life pursuit should be warily chosen and seldom abandoned. One who can not succeed in a business he understands is

almost sure to fail in one he does not
understand.   In his ignorance, and com-
peting with skill arising from experience, how can he win success?   Men
must arise by elevating, not by abandoning their several industries.   Normal
successes of life are attained by faithful
use of native and acquired skill, and
the opportunities ever offered to intelli-
gent industry.   The rising generation
should be taught to abide in their calling
and identify their hopes with its prosperity.   People leaving farms, shops and
offices to speculate in oil wells, mines,
or town lots have demoralized labor
and plunged thousands into the discontents, temptations, and miseries of
poverty.

XXVI.

A SHIP starting on a year's voyage
with only stores for a month may
glide cheerily over smooth seas, taking
no account of the future. But when
storms tatter her sails, yawning seas
open to engulf her creaking hull, and
bread and water fail, starvation breeds
mutiny and at the first port crew
and voyagers will abandon the unpro-
visioned ship. Inadequate intellectual
and moral stores account for much of
the disappointment and misery of later
years of life. Diversions of thoughtless
childhood and giddy youth mock the

wants of riper years as stale provisions or empty casks and larders despairing voyagers. The average child embarks on the voyage of life as a ship with scanty provisions, doomed to the misery of want and discontent. Without mastery of passions, discipline of affections, culture of intellect, and established principles, no life can be happy and honorable. These accomplishments give contentment and· dignity to manhood, serenity and hope to old age! William E. Dodge asked a discouraged young man seeking help in an emergency, " Do you drink ? " "Never." " Smoke ? " " I never use tobacco." " Do you gamble ? " " I don't know the use of cards. I have other tastes and associations. I am superintendent of a Sunday School." The merchant, with eyes filled with tears, at the remembrance of aid given him by the young man's father after asking the same questions thirty years before, gave him the needed help and saved his credit and business. "I have been young and now I am old, and yet I have not seen the righteous forsaken nor his seed begging bread." Let every child be furnished with Christian tastes, principles and habits before confided to the uncertainties and perils of the voyage of life! There is no greater crime against humanity than for parents and teachers to send forth into the ways of life the ignorant and vicious to prey upon the public welfare. There is no greater benefactor of the republic than he who trains for her true men and women.

"Behold, thou art pilot of the ship and owner of the freighted galleon, .
Competent with all the weakness to steer in safety or be lost."

XXVII.

SAILS.

To make the quickest time all sails must sometimes be used, top and top gallant sails, and even studding sails expanded from the ship's side as the wing of a bird to catch the faintest breath of a dying breeze. American vessels are the swiftest on the seas, not from superior model chiefly, but from carrying more sail. Other vessels spread an amount of canvas the ship may safely bear without frequent change. They avoid the care and labor of frequent unfurling and furling sails, with the varying winds. American ships

crowd on canvas to avail themselves
of the least and most transient breeze,
and hasten into port leaving less industrious sailors flapping their canvas
in a calm, or driven from their course
by a storm. Those on life's voyage
making the most of present advantages
are ever leaving behind them the in-
dolent and the careless. Francis Joseph
Campbell, a blind man, became a distinguished mathematician, musician, and
philanthropist. When complimented for
his proficiency in so many pursuits his
wife replied: "The difference between
him and all other people I know is, he
makes use of all his opportunities."
Promptness in seizing them is a secret
of success.

"Timeliness in being at the right spot
in every emergency," Emerson thinks,
"is sometimes more important than

industry or frugality!" One losing no opportunity is almost sure of promotion. He is likely to be wanted for some place of trust or partnership and soon be ranked with the employers or capitalists. Neglecting advantages offered to the earlier periods of life leaves manhood unprovided for and beclouds old age with want and sorrow. A lad obtained employment as an office-boy in New York at four dollars a week. He had no advantages but capacity, industry, faithfulness, love of books, and a fine instinct of economy. He rose year after year in rank of service and in salary, till he is the manager of the largest manufacturing establishment of the kind in the world, receives perhaps a larger salary than any bank or railroad officer in the country. Though not much over forty,

C. S. has been Mayor of the second largest city of a Commonwealth, and is distinguished as a cultured gentleman and a Christian benefactor. Opportunities are among the talents dispensed to men whose neglect brings guilt and disaster, but whose faithful and wary use gains favor in Heaven and enlarged dominion on earth. Tripping or loitering on the course, one will be a laggard at the goal. The ship gaining port and winning from others prizes of the market, watched winds and currents, vigilantly maintained her course, and crowded sail.

> "There is a tide in the affairs of men,
>   Which, taken at the flood, leads on to fortune;
>   Omitted, all the voyage of their life
>   Is bound in shallows, and in miseries."

XXVIII.

CHART.

CHARTS of the seas have been drawn, revised, and perfected through the observations of the navigators of the ages. Boundaries of continents, location of islands, direction of Gulf Streams, and prevailing winds, dangerous and safe roads of the sea, lighthouses guiding entrance into ports, are all mapped down. Navigation no more ignores these waymarks of the sea, than travel the highways of continents. Without a chart a ship might beat about near a port, uncertain of her position and afraid to enter. Disregarding these waymarks of

the sea, one runs greater hazards than in
discarding the public roads in crossing a
continent. The experiences, traditions,
and moral teachings of religious dispensa-
tions summarized in Divine Revelation
distinguish all the safe paths of life.
The Bible is a universal directory of
human conduct. One accepting its guidance escapes the sunken reefs of error,
the Gulf Stream of false philosophy, and
the storm-swept roads of sensualism,
and safely reaches the port of happy
destiny. On a New England sea-board
was born of poor parents a sickly child.
At the age of nine he was cook on
a fishing smack. At eleven he sailed
as cabin boy in a whaler. He was
addicted to the vices of seamen till he
was thirty-four, without any earnest care
or ambition for his future. But the
religious instinct indestructible in his

ardent Welsh nature at length disturbed his peace, and awakened foreboding apprehensions.   He read his long-neglected Bible, partly to ease his conscience and partly for argument with shipmates. The Divine Word fastened itself in his memory, quickened his conscience, and rooted itself in his heart.   After sharp struggle in penitence and prayer, he became a joyful believer and won shipmates to his new-found faith.

He conducted prayer meetings in the forecastle.   His office as mate and afterward as captain gave prestige to his Bible readings and exhortations.   Revivals followed at sea, and were reported in Bethel magazines, and Ebenezer Morgan became known as the Christian Sea Captain.   Since leaving the sea he has been heard with interest in pulpits throughout the land.   While rising in

Christian reputation he was accumulating means through successful whaling voyages. He was the first man to hoist the American flag in Alaska after its cession to the United States, and in organizing the seal fishery in that territory. His increasing means have been spent in private and Christian charities, founding churches, supporting missions. Appreciating from his own experience the Bible as the world's religious guide, and seeking to exalt its supremacy and protect its integrity, he accepted the presidency of the American and Foreign Bible Society, purchased the best Biblical library in the world, for help to future revision of the Scriptures, in all languages, and became an important factor in a new plan of Bible work adopted by a great denomination. Having found the Bible the best chart for himself, he would publish it for all voyagers of life. Following the sea without a chart is no more foolhardy and hazardous than adventuring upon the casual life of selfishness and sin without accepted examples, precedents and sanctions. "Wherewith shall a young man cleanse his way? By taking heed thereto according to Thy Word." The young man or woman should be as familiar with the Decalogue and Proverbs and the Sermon on the Mount as with streets of their native city or roads intersecting their native town.

"Compass and chart are in thy hand; roadsted and rock thou knowest.

"Thou art warned of reefs and shallows; thou beholdest the harbor and its lights."

XXIX.

THE mariner no longer guides his bark
by projecting coastlines, or by shifting
clouds, or uncertain light of stars,
nor does he fear to direct his course
across unknown seas. The compass,
pointing ever to the North Pole, fur-
nishes the same safe guidance for voyagers through all ages. But to assure
accurate direction, allowance must be
made for variations of the needle in
different longitudes. Overlooking this
subtle bias, a ship might lose her
course and miss her port. A traitor,
it is related, betrayed his country's fleet

by concealing a loadstone near the compass. When they supposed they had arrived at their native shores, they were landed on a hostile coast. Conscience guides the voyage of life to its moral destiny. It is an inner law, which no revision of expediency nor reckless defiance can . wholly pervert, or extirpate. Yet it is subjected to such subtle influences of interest, passion, education, or of public opinion, that often its guidance should be challenged. Paul was conscientious in persecuting the Churches. Devotees of false faiths are doubtless sincere. Millions on the voyage of life, making no allowance for variations of conscience, are sailing on dangerous seas, and liable to be wrecked on unknown coasts. A biased conscience precipitates or apologizes for all the false aims and pursuits of life. Religious sects, however divergent in their doctrine and discipline, profess to sail by the same compass. "There is a way that seemeth right unto a man, but the end thereof are the ways of death!" For weal, or woe, man must follow his conscience in moral history and destiny. The true conscience is conformed to the perfect law of God—

"True as the needle to the pole
His steadfast heart is bent."

XXX.

WITHOUT a helm there can be no safe navigation of the seas. A rudderless craft is liable to drift from her course by any current, be capsized by any flaw of wind, or driven a wreck upon any sunken reef or rocky shore. A hand is always at the helm, from the moment a ship leaves one port till she is moored in another. In any crisis of peril, the value of sails, service of seamen, or compass even depends upon a power at the helm. A determined will is the helmsman in the voyage of life. The value of talents, opportunities, or patronage, depends upon self-government. Any increase of advantages without it is an increase of power for evil. It is like the force of steam that, uncontrolled, may produce disaster. As more attention may be necessary to hold a ship's course in a calm, over smooth waters, than in a gale, through rough seas; so greater temptations arise in intervals of business or seasons of recreation, than amid intensest professional or industrial engagements. Employment is always safer than idleness or leisure. While industrious sons of poverty are rising in wealth and position, the unoccupied heirs of fortune are losing their estates, and becoming effeminate and vicious. Without a purpose there can be no self-government. Without self-government, life is a rudderless

bark drifting on some unknown shore.
Self-government is the self-possession
of a commander on the eve of a battle; of a captain in the crisis of a gale;
of an engineer hazarding his life to in-
sure the safety of the train; or of unruf-
fled temper amid business annoyances,
or under provoking insult. A clerical
friend, flagrantly insulted at the polls,
by a distinguished politician excited by
the heat of the canvass as well as by
the cup, calmly fixed the attention of
bystanders and remarked in a quiet
but emphatic manner, "Sir, no gentleman will insult me, no other can!"
The hero of self-conquest is greater
than the captor of a city, the con-
queror of a country, or the founder
of a kingdom. Mastery of one's self
makes one superior to all adversaries
and adverse influences. Lack of it

exposes one to all the temptations and antagonisms of the world.

"Leave the rudder awhile to swing round, give the
    wind its heading and be lost,
Stand bold to thy tiller, guide thee by the pole star
    and be safe."

XXXI.

THE anchor holds a ship against wind, current, or tide. No vessel is furnished for sea without it. The safety of cargo, crew and passengers often depends upon it. An anchor with its cable coiled around it in hold or on the fore deck of the ship is scarcely noticed. But on a dangerous coast, or entering port, all appreciate the security it gives. What more interesting spectacle than a ship, returned from a long voyage, lying at anchor in the bay, and waiting to be warped into her moorings!

Hope is the anchor of life's voyager.

Through experiences of prosperity he is scarcely conscious of its ministry in multiplying incentives to industry, cheering pursuits of life, and reconciling to its adversities. Says John Bright—" One of the most painful things to my mind, to be seen in England, is this, that among the classes which earn their living, by their daily labor, there is an absence of that hope, which every man ought to have, if he is industrious and frugal, of a comfortable independence as he advances in life." In the emergencies and trials of life, and approach of death, hope is a ministering angel. The Christian hope is the climax of the most ennobling aspirations of humanity. It soars and sings over the sorrows of bereavement and death, and the darkness of the grave; and rejoices in anticipation of a perfected destiny in heaven. It is a staff for the pilgrim through the valley and shadow of death; a light streaming from the gate of the celestial city to guide his doubtful footsteps; a song of welcome cheering his dreary passage over the Jordan of death.

> " And through the storm and dangerous thrall
> It led me to the Port of Peace."

XXXII.

In crossing the ocean a voyager may encounter Gulf Stream, iceberg, sunken reef, or stormy cape. He may pass roads of the sea distinguished by traditions of wreck and disaster. Certain periods and circumstances of life are beset with special temptations and perils. After long prevalence of adverse winds sometimes vessels are seen hovering near and seeking to double some cape. After turning that point the wind would be favorable and waft them into their desired haven. So noble barks of youth hover around

turning points in the voyage of life.
If they can pass safely the dangers of
leaving home, forming new companion-
ships, choosing a business, or settlement
in a city, prosperity and honor are assured! Many never pass these dangerous capes, but buffeted by storms
finally sink in waters of oblivion.
Some, bearing up against adverse
winds, at length make the dangerous
passage, and reach a peaceful haven.
Amid these perils guardian influences
are available to those who seek them.
The petrel does not appear when sky
is clear, wind low, and sea smooth.
But when the storm howls through
the rigging, waves beat over the ship,
it hovers near, following the imperiled
vessel through the storm, now beating
her prow, now her stern, and anon
her sides, with tireless wings. In the

beautiful superstition of seamen, they are the souls of departed sailors, hovering near their former comrades in peril. Amid the heaving billows of temptation, let memories of childhood, home, parents, brothers, and sisters, hover around as guardian angels. Let a sainted mother smile upon virtuous purposes and deeds, and frown sorrowfully upon thoughts and acts of evil. Let the counsels and prayers of a venerated father be recalled to cheer and support you in uprightness. Above all, remember the watchful eye of God.

"If the friends who embraced thee in prosperity's
  glow,
With a smile for each joy and a tear for each
  woe,
Should forsake thee when tempted, and clouds are
  arrayed;
Look aloft to the friendship that never shall fade.

" In the tempest of life wnen the wave and the gale
Are around and above, if thy footing should fail,
If thine eye should grow dim, or thy courage de-
    part;
Look aloft and be firm and fearless of heart."

XXXIII.

LOG-BOOK.

THE record of a voyage is kept, with frequent calculations of the latitude, longitude, and progress of the ship. Through the study of this record the vessel's speed, course, distance from port, and position on the sea may be ascertained at any time, and the safety and success of the voyage assured. By the study of personal, or other's experience, as narrated in the lives of successful men, double assurance may be gained for a prosperous and happy life. Confucius illustrated to his pupils the dangers of inexperience

by showing them how sportsmen
snared only young birds straying from
nests and brooding care of the old
birds. Premature removal from guardian care of home betrays thousands
into prodigal life. Half the failures
in business or profession might have
been averted by heeding lessons of
personal or parental experience. It
were safer for one to tear up the
record of his voyage, throw away his
map, and remain ignorant of his place
on the seas, than take no account of
his religious convictions and experience.
A man having no regard for his
higher relations and destinies, nor ex-
amining his motives and principles, can
never feel sure that he is true to himself, to man, or to God! By wary
study of one's faults he may often
make them stepping-stones to success,

turning defeats into victories. Be then
in knowledge and mastery of thyself

" As a pilot well expert in perilous waves,
That to a steadfast star his course has bent."

XXXIV.

BOUTING SHIP.

A SHIP unable to sail against a head-wind beats against it by varying her course. This changing course is "tacking ship." It is an exciting scene—sailors on deck and hands on ropes—command given—ropes pulled and helm turned—and sails sweep around and secure the wind over the opposite quarter. Now the ship moves majestically toward her destined port. Conversion is the moral voyager bouting ship. In natural depravity his helm is set away from heaven; and his sails, swelled by gales of passion, bear him toward the gulf of perdition. Every human being must experience a radical change of heart, purpose, motives, and habits, to attain eternal life. The learned Pharisee, zealous champion of the common faith, and bitter persecutor of the despised Nazarene, cheering on murderers of the first martyr of the new faith, having been arrested by a voice from heaven, authenticated to him by a supernatural light, changed the whole purpose and conduct of his life, and became next to its founder the mightiest upbuilder of the faith he had sought to destroy. This is but a conspicuous example of the Christian regeneration in all lands and ages. Christian churches are filled by those claiming a corresponding change in their motives and principles of life. The only way for voyagers drifting

with currents of selfishness or driven
by storms of passion and temptation
out of their course is to "bout ship."
Hope dawns only in change of heart
and life.

> " Deep horror then my vitals froze,
>   Death struck. I ceased the tide to stem,
> When suddenly a star arose,
>   It was the Star of Bethlehem."

XXXV.

In navigating the seas there are auguries of the close of the voyage. Green waters reveal approach to mainland. Spicy breezes proclaim proximity of islands of the Indian Ocean. New varieties of sea weed floating about his ships assured Columbus the shores of a New World were near. So gray hairs, loss of appetite, sleep, and hope, portend the close of life. How forboding that close to many! Chesterfield, the exemplar of the world's fashion and honor, in the review of life said: "I have known all the pleasures of this world and conse-

quently know their futility and do not
regret their loss. I appraise them at their
real value, which is very low. I look
upon all that is past as one of those ro-
mantic dreams that opium commonly oc-
casions, and I do not by any means
desire to repeat the nauseous dose for
the sake of the fugitive dream." How
bitter Byron's lament over his brilliant
career!

"Alas, for myself, so dark my fate
  Through every turn of life hath been,
Man and the world so much I hate
  I care not when I quit the scene.
My days are in the yellow leaf,
  The flowers and fruit of love are gone,
The worm the canker and the grief
  Are mine alone."

Madame Maintenon, the most popular
woman at the French court, bewails the
vanity of a worldly life. " I have been

young and beautiful, have had a relish of pleasures, and have been the universal object of love. In a more advanced age I spent years in intellectual pleasures. I have at least risen to favor, but I protest that every one of these conditions leaves the mind a dismal vacancy." A friend was asked: "How is your class-mate doing?" "Not very well, I am sorry to say." "Why, I thought I heard he was about the top of the profession!" "So he is." "And growing rich fast?" "Yes, that is true." "Well, what do you mean?" "I mean that he is running down hill every day, and is now almost at the bottom. He seemed to be a noble fellow in college, with something of almost Christian principle in him. But he sogged away into a mean ambition, growing harder and colder with every year, is getting more tightly hidebound in his selfishness, and, for aught I see, is already virtually a lost man." The end of every worldly career alike is found after the fullest experience of its votaries a failure. Those living in any worldly passion or pursuit are "dead while they live" and hasten to the oblivion and shame of a wasted life. In contrast to the heroes of the world the Apostle exclaims, " I have fought the good fight, kept the faith, and finished the course, and henceforth there is laid up for me a crown of life; and not for me only, but for all that wait for His appearing."

" Thanks be to God who giveth us the victory through our Lord Jesus Christ." However various their life, the end of the righteous is alike blessed. He hears the plaudit, " Well done, good and faithful servant, enter thou into the joy of thy

Lord." "Let me die the death of the righteous and let my last end be like his," is the importunate prayer of humanity awaking to its most urgent necessities.

XXXVI.

THE HAVEN.

In Coles' "Voyage of Life" the artist represents, in a series of pictures, the progress, perils, and peaceful close of human life. In the first picture the child appears in a little boat emerging from the source of a mountain stream. Flowers brighten the hills, heap the boat and enwreath the cherub's limbs as he leaps up to greet the smiling world. To show the affiliation of childhood with the history and destinies of the race, human heads are carved on the boat. To mark the periods of life an hour-glass rises from the prow. To

symbolize a guardian Providence an
angel stands at the helm. In the next
picture a youth appears in presumptuous
self-reliance grieving away the guardian
angel which hovers near with anxious
look. Grasping the helm he gazes
hopefully at the temple of fame looming
up in the distance to direct and cheer
his course. But the turn in the stream
just before him leading over perilous
rapids towards an unseen cataract escapes his attention! In the third picture
the bark has been drawn upon the
dangerous rapids before unseen, but
the guardian angel still, disregarded
and grieved farther away, peers out of
distant clouds watching the reckless
and imperiled voyager. In despair he
has now abandoned the helm and is
waiting in sullen gloom the catastrophe,
as the boat dashes down the impetuous

torrent. In the last picture the old man is emerging into a boundless sea. As the measurement of time has ceased, the hour-glass has fallen from the prow of his boat. As self-direction has ended, the helm is broken from the stern. Rejoicing in contrition for sin and restored faith in the Fatherhood of God, the angelic guardian has returned to guide the penitent believer into the Heavenly Rest. From parting heavens angels are descending upon beams of light to welcome the time-worn voyager to the Everlasting Haven! A ship returns from a voyage around the world, canvas blackened, rigging chafed, and worn, some of the crew lost, riding outside the harbor, waiting to be warped into her moorings. What seas she has traversed! What perils past! What storms have howled through her cordage and

plunged her beneath the waves! What
billows swept her deck and tossed her
as a feather! She seems a thing of life,
with heart throbbing with the courage
of her victories and sympathy with her
voyagers. The sea seems lighted up
with smiles at her safe return! This is
an image of the close of the Christian's
life. He has traversed wide seas of experience. Sometimes becalmed, sometimes driven before a gale, sometimes
appearing hopelessly wrecked, he is in
port at last! Providing sufficient stores,
carefully studying chart, clinging to helm,
and skillfully using sails, anchor, and log-
book, he has reached the blessed haven.
What rapture attends the close of a
prosperous voyage! O! the shout when
land appears—native shore, city, familiar
spire, home of childhood!

"Once on the raging seas I rode,
　　The storm was loud, the night was dark;
　The ocean yawned and rudely blowed
　　The wind that tossed my foundering bark.

But rescued from all perils of sin he out-
rode the stormy seas.

"There safely moored, my perils o'er,
　　I'll sing in night's diadem,
　For ever and for evermore
　　The star, the star of Bethlehem."